The End of the RAINBOW

Liza Donnelly

Holiday House / New York

Copyright © 2015 by Liza Donnelly
All Rights Reserved
HOLIDAY HOUSE is registered in the U.S. Patent and Trademark Office.
Printed and Bound in October 2014 at Toppan Leefung, DongGuan City, China.
The artwork was created with pen and ink and watercolor.
www.holidayhouse.com
First Edition
1 3 5 7 9 10 8 6 4 2

Library of Congress Cataloging-in-Publication Data
Donnelly, Liza, author, illustrator.
The end of the rainbow / Liza Donnelly. — First edition.
pages cm. — (I like to read)
Summary: "While looking for the end of the rainbow, a girl finds
something even better: new friends"— Provided by publisher.
ISBN 978-0-8234-3291-2 (hardcover)
[1. Rainbows—Fiction. 2. Friendship—Fiction.] I. Title.
PZ7.D7195End 2015
[E]—dc23
2014023459

ISBN 978-0-8234-3396-4 (paperback)

To my father, who taught me how to go on adventures

I love the rain.

Wow! A rainbow!

What do you think is at the end?

Let's go see.

Look. A rabbit!

We are going to the end
of the rainbow.

Do you want to come?

Look. A bird!

We are going to the end
of the rainbow.

Do you want to come?

Hi, Turtle! We are going
to the end of the rainbow.
Do you want to come?

Hello, Horse! We are going
to the end of the rainbow.
Do you want to come?

I can't wait to get there!

It's gone.

That's okay.

We didn't find the end
of the rainbow.

But we found something better.

We found new friends!

You will like these too!

Come Back, Ben by Ann Hassett and John Hassett
A *Kirkus Reviews* Best Book

Dinosaurs Don't, Dinosaurs Do by Steve Björkman
A Notable Social Studies Trade Book for Young People
An IRA/CBC Children's Choice

Fish Had a Wish by Michael Garland
A *Kirkus Reviews* Best Book
A Top 25 Children's Books list book

The Fly Flew In by David Catrow
An IRA/CBC Children's Choice
Maryland Blue Crab Young Reader Award Winner

Look! by Ted Lewin
The Correll Book Award for Excellence
in Early Childhood Informational Text

Me Too! by Valeri Gorbachev
A Bank Street Best Children's Book of the Year

Mice on Ice by Rebecca Emberley and Ed Emberley
A Bank Street Best Children's Book of the Year
An IRA/CBC Children's Choice

Pig Has a Plan by Ethan Long
An IRA/CBC Children's Choice

See Me Dig by Paul Meisel
A *Kirkus Reviews* Best Book

See Me Run by Paul Meisel
A Theodor Seuss Geisel Award Honor Book
An ALA Notable Children's Book

You Can Do It! by Betsy Lewin
A Bank Street Best Children's Book of the Year,
Outstanding Merit

See more I Like to Read® books.
Go to www.holidayhouse.com/I-Like-to-Read/